Dear Parents and Educators,

Welcome to Penguin Young Readers! As parents and educators, you know that each child develops at his or her own pace—in terms of speech, critical thinking, and, of course, reading. Penguin Young Readers recognizes this fact. As a result, each Penguin Young Readers book is assigned a traditional easy-to-read level (1–4) as well as a Guided Reading Level (A–P). Both of these systems will help you choose the right book for your child. Please refer to the back of each book for specific leveling information. Penguin Young Readers features esteemed authors and illustrators, stories about favorite characters, fascinating nonfiction, and more!

| Power Rangers: Ninja Steel
The Legend of Ninja Steel | LEVEL **3**
GUIDED READING LEVEL **M** |

This book is perfect for a **Transitional Reader** who:
- can read multisyllable and compound words;
- can read words with prefixes and suffixes;
- is able to identify story elements (beginning, middle, end, plot, setting, characters, problem, solution); and
- can understand different points of view.

Here are some **activities** you can do during and after reading this book:
- Character Traits: Come up with a list of words to describe each Power Ranger. For example, Calvin is described as "silly."
- Creative Writing: Master Dane has retrieved the Ninja Nexus Prism and asks you, a Power Ranger, to guard it. How will you protect the Prism? Write a paragraph describing your plan to keep it out of the hands of the evil Galvanax.

Remember, sharing the love of reading with a child is the best gift you can give!

—Sarah Fabiny, Editorial Director
 Penguin Young Readers program

*Penguin Young Readers are leveled by independent reviewers applying the standards developed by Irene Fountas and Gay Su Pinnell in *Matching Books to Readers: Using Leveled Books in Guided Reading*, Heinemann, 1999.

PENGUIN YOUNG READERS
An Imprint of Penguin Random House LLC

ISBN 9780515159769   10 9 8 7 6 5 4 3 2

THE LEGEND OF NINJA STEEL

by Max Bisantz

SABAN Brands

Penguin Young Readers
An Imprint of Penguin Random House

Glossary

Galaxy Warriors is the name of a game show. Monsters battle to prove who is the mightiest warrior.

Galvanax is the name of an evil alien fighter. He created the game show *Galaxy Warriors* and wants to destroy Earth.

Madame Odius is one of Galvanax's evil helpers.

Ninja Nexus Prism is a magic crystal that finds worthy fighters and helps them battle against evil.

Ninja Nexus Star is the strongest weapon ever known. Whoever has the star can turn into a Power Ranger.

Ninja Power Stars are powerful weapons created from broken pieces of the Ninja Nexus Star.

Ninja Steel is the powerful metal crust that protects the Ninja Nexus Prism.

Ripcon is another one of Galvanax's evil helpers.

Ten years ago, something strange fell from the sky. Master Dane and his sons, Brody and Aiden, had never seen anything like it.

The object was still smoking when Master Dane brought it indoors. He carefully chipped away at the hard metal crust to see what was inside. This crust was Ninja Steel.

Master Dane saw that the strange object was shaped like a ninja throwing star. This was the Ninja Nexus Prism. Inside the Prism was a colorful star called the Ninja Nexus Star.

Dane did not know how powerful these objects were. But he knew that they had fallen to Earth for a reason.

In his spaceship high above
Earth, Galvanax and his evil crew
wanted the Ninja Nexus Prism for
themselves. They would do anything
to control it. They traveled down to
Earth to take it back from Master
Dane.

Galvanax kidnapped Brody
to lure Master Dane out of his
workshop. Master Dane ran to his
son's rescue.

"Let Brody go," he said bravely.

"You're surrounded," Galvanax
replied.

Madame Odius and Ripcon
suddenly appeared. Master Dane
and Brody had nowhere to hide.

"Now give me the Ninja Nexus Star," Galvanax ordered.

"You can't give it to him, Dad," Brody said.

"He has no choice!" Galvanax
screamed. Galvanax fired a wave of
energy at Master Dane. But Dane
used the Ninja Nexus Star to protect
himself. Then, something strange
happened.

Master Dane morphed into the Red Power Ranger!

"The legend is true," Madame Odius said. "He's become a Power Ranger."

Galvanax and Master Dane battled. But Master Dane was struck by a terrible explosion and fell to the ground. Galvanax took hold of the Ninja Nexus Star. He was becoming more powerful by the second.

"That star came to me so I can protect it from evil like you!" Master Dane said. He lifted himself off the ground and ran at Galvanax. He used his sword to cut through the Ninja Nexus Star.

BOOM!

There was a huge explosion.
When the smoke cleared, Master
Dane was gone! In his place was the
Ninja Nexus Prism. Brody looked
into the Prism and saw the broken
pieces of the Nexus Star transform
into six Ninja Power Stars.

"Back off!" Galvanax shouted at Brody. "They're mine!" But Galvanax could not break through the Prism.

"I'll find a way to get those stars out," the monster said. "Bring the Prism to the ship. And put that brat in chains!"

Ripcon grabbed Brody, and the aliens took their captive into outer space.

Galvanax created a show called
Galaxy Warriors. Monsters fought
each other. Whichever monster won
could try to pull a Ninja Power Star
out of the Prism. No one could do it.

Galvanax did not know that only true Power Rangers could reach inside the Prism. He was never destined to control the Ninja Power Stars. But five ordinary teenagers were . . .

After ten years in space, Brody finally escapes back to Earth. Brody has the power to morph into the Red Ranger and protect the world from evil monsters like Galvanax.

He hopes to reunite with his brother and father, Aiden and Master Dane.

Preston has the power to control
the Blue Ninja Power Star and
morph into the Blue Ranger. He
comes from a wealthy family in the
small town of Summer Cove.

Preston is a star student at Summer Cove High School. He loves magic tricks and hopes to become a world-class magician when he gets older. He uses his Ninja Star powers for good.

Hayley is an adventurous teenager who loves the outdoors. She often goes on long walks with her dog, Kodiak. Hayley has the power to morph into the White Ranger.

Hayley wants to make the world a better place by protecting it from villains. She hopes to become a politician one day and continue to help the community.

Calvin loves building motorcycles and cars. His yellow truck is named Nitro. He is one of the coolest kids at Summer Cove High School. Calvin has the power to morph into the Yellow Ranger.

Calvin can be a bit silly, and he is not used to working hard. Being a Power Ranger is a lot of hard work, and Calvin has a lot to learn!

Sarah is the brains behind the Power Rangers. She has control of the Pink Ninja Power Star and can morph into the Pink Ranger.

Sarah loves the thrill of going fast and enjoys high-speed trains. She wants to be an engineer when she grows up.

All five teenagers will become
the true masters of the Ninja Power
Stars. But Galvanax will never stop
fighting to control them himself. He
is determined to be the most feared
ruler in the galaxy.

Galvanax even sends monsters from *Galaxy Warriors* down to Earth to battle the Power Rangers. So far, no one has beat the Rangers.

The legend of Ninja Steel began long, long ago. But the future is uncertain.

Brody, Preston, Sarah, Hayley, and Calvin don't know why they were chosen to become Power Rangers. Perhaps the Ninja Power Stars chose them. But they know how important it is to protect the Ninja Power Stars and keep them away from evil villains.